Mama Outside, Mama Inside

Dianna Hutts Aston ～ illustrated by **Susan Gaber**

Henry Holt and Company ～ New York

*Special thanks to my avian spies, Candy Champion Hutts
and Pauline Tom, Mountain City's "Bluebird Lady."* —D. H. A.

Henry Holt and Company, LLC, *Publishers since 1866*
175 Fifth Avenue, New York, New York 10010 [www.henryholtchildrensbooks.com]

Henry Holt® is a registered trademark of Henry Holt and Company, LLC.
Text copyright © 2006 by Dianna Hutts Aston. Illustrations copyright © 2006 by Susan Gaber
All rights reserved. Distributed in Canada by H. B. Fenn and Company Ltd.

Library of Congress Cataloging-in-Publication Data
Aston, Dianna Hutts.
Mama Outside, Mama Inside / Dianna Hutts Aston ; illustrated by Susan Gaber.—1st ed.
p.   cm.
Summary: Two mothers—a human and a bird—prepare for the birth of their babies while living very close to each other.
ISBN-13: 978-0-8050-7716-2 / ISBN-10: 0-8050-7716-2
[1. Mother and child—Fiction. 2. Pregnancy—Fiction. 3. Birds—Fiction.] I. Gaber, Susan, ill. II. Title.
PZ7.A92233Mam 2006   [E]—dc22   2005012725

First Edition—2006 / Designed by Patrick Collins
The artist used acrylic paint on Bristol board to create the illustrations for this book.
Printed in China

1 3 5 7 9 10 8 6 4 2

To my aunt, Diane Champion Mullins,
who knows how to feather a nest
and make things bloom
—D. H. A.

For Laraine and Bill
—S. G.

The babies are coming!
The mamas have so much
to do before they arrive.

Mama Outside finds just the right spot
for a nest.

Mama Inside finds just the right room
for a nursery.

Mama Outside weaves the nest
with things Daddy has found.

Mama Inside knits a blanket
as Daddy paints the nursery.

Mama Outside makes her nest soft
with rootlets, moss, and leaves as delicate
as angel wings.

Mama Inside makes the cradle cozy with
a cushion, a lamb, and a blanket the color
of sunshine.

Now everything is ready.

Mama Outside lays her
eggs and snuggles with
them while Daddy sings.

Mama Inside feels her baby
stretching and turning inside
when Daddy sings.

Days pass.

Days and days.

Waiting days.

Then one bright morning,
Mama Outside feels tiny
bump-bump-bumps...

...as her babies
peck-peck-peck
until their shells
crick-crick-cra-*a-ack!*

"Cheep? Cheep!
Cheep-cheep-cheep!"
cry the babies.

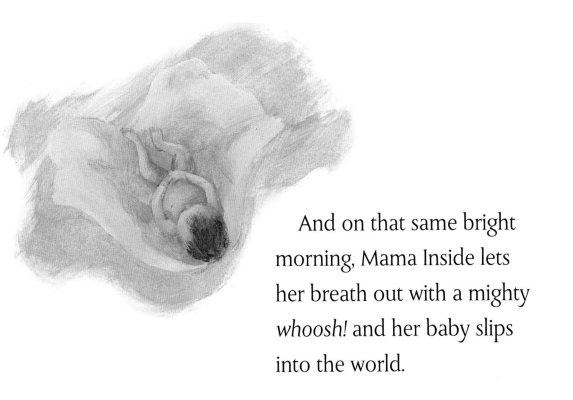

And on that same bright morning, Mama Inside lets her breath out with a mighty *whoosh!* and her baby slips into the world.

"Waaa-waaa-waaa!" cries the baby.

Mama Outside welcomes her babies
with songs and gentle pecks.

Mama Inside welcomes her baby
with laughter and lots of kisses.

And oh, those hungry babies!

Mama Outside feeds her babies tasty insects and juicy berries all through the day and all through the night. Daddy helps.

Mama Inside gives her baby her milk all through the day and all through the night. Daddy helps.

Mama Outside listens to the cooing
on the other side of the window. . .
and coos to her babies.

Mama Inside listens to the singing
on the other side of the window . . .
and sings to her baby.

Days pass.

Days and days.

Growing days.

The time has come for Mama Outside to teach
her babies how to spread their wings and fly.

Mama Inside holds her baby
up to the window to watch.

Mama Outside looks at Mama Inside and tilts her head just so.

Mama Inside smiles at Mama Outside and says, "Good-bye, good bird. Good Mama Bird."

Then Mama Outside follows
her babies into the sky.

And Mama Inside rocks until long after her baby has gone to sleep.

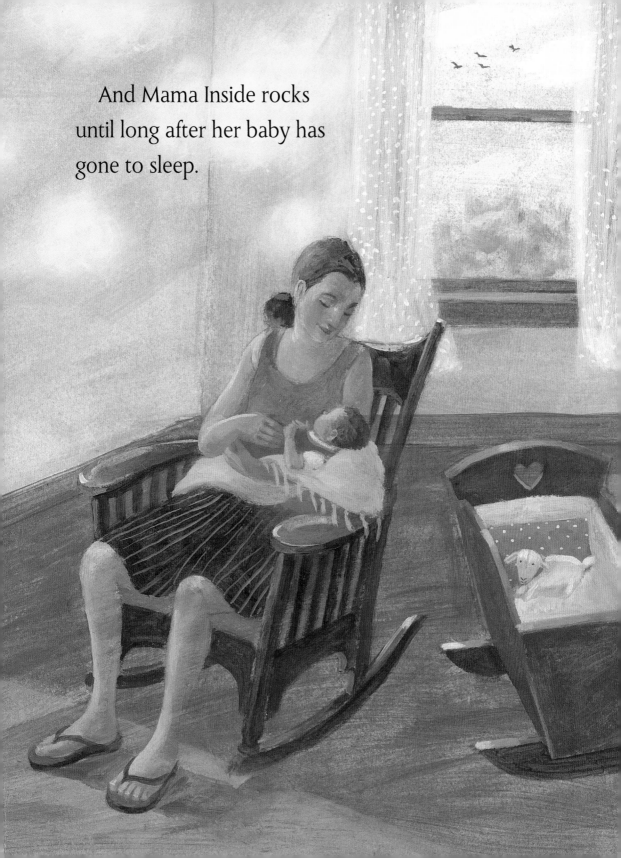